The WOLF who LEARNED to Be Good

Natalia Moore

Albert Whitman & Company
Chicago, Illinois

In a lonely wood, there lived a wolf.

A rather naughty wolf.

Everyone knows wolves are very big and very bad—they just can't help themselves!

But Wolf was not like other wolves. He actually wanted to be good.

Being well-behaved was not easy for a wicked wolf.
He tried and he tried. Nothing worked.

Good Lesson *number 10*

Throw your friends a surprise party!

It was quite lonely being a big bad wolf.

"What happens if I never, ever make a friend of my very own?" the wolf grumbled.

"What's the matter?" asked a little girl in a pink beret.
She smelled of honey and cinnamon.

"I want to have a friend to play with," sobbed the wolf.
He opened his eyes and saw the little girl. She looked delicious!

Wolf couldn't help but think of all the
wicked ways he could gobble her up.

Fry her with onions and a dash of oil.

Boil her in a delicious broth.

Bake her in a cake.

The wolf's mouth
watered with hunger.

The girl had other ideas. She opened up her
bag of wonders and got to work on Wolf.

She gave him a makeover
to cheer him up.

She braided his hair so he
wouldn't look so scruffy.

Wolf was having so much fun that he totally forgot
he had planned to gobble the girl up in one go.

Then she took some cookies from her bag.

"Give them to me!" snapped the wolf and he devoured every last one.

"Get me a drink!" he demanded and licked his chops.

"Do you want to play school?" she asked politely.

"No! We have to play my games!" he boomed.

"Then I'll play on my own!" said the girl glumly.
"Friends. Who needs them? I can have fun all
by myself," said Wolf.

But it wasn't fun.
It was boring!
Wolf turned an
odd shade of red.
He had a rather
strange feeling,
a guilty feeling.

He plodded over to the girl and tapped her on the shoulder.

"Sorry," he said sheepishly.

The girl gave him a big hug, and they played with her toys.

She even let Wolf play with Mr. Fudge—her most favorite toy!

It was getting late and the girl needed to go home.
So she picked up her bag and put Mr. Fudge in her pocket.
Wolf took her to the edge of the lonely wood, so she
didn't have far to go on her own.
She gave Wolf a big squeeze and waved good-bye.

In a lonely wood, there lives a wolf.

A rather good wolf.

A rather good wolf who made a friend.

A wolf, who is good...

most of the time!

Library of Congress Cataloging-in-Publication data is on file with the publisher.

Text and pictures copyright © 2017 by Natalia Moore
Published in 2017 by Albert Whitman & Company
ISBN 978-0-8075-9204-5

Printed in China
10 9 8 7 6 5 4 3 2 1 HH 22 21 20 19 18 17

Design by Jordan Kost

For more information about Albert Whitman & Company,
visit our website at www.albertwhitman.com.